3/17

THUD & BLUNDER

Thud and Blunder is published by Stone Arch Books,
A Capstone Imprint
1710 Roe Crest Drive
North Mankato, Minnesota 56003
www.mycapstone.com

Cataloging-in-Publication Data is available at the
Library of Congress website.
ISBN: 978-1-4965-3219-0 (library binding)
ISBN: 978-1-4965-3223-7 (paperback)
ISBN: 978-1-4965-3227-5 (eBook PDF)

Summary: Thud and Blunder join a dance-loving knight
on a quest for fame and fortune.

Printed in the USA
009658CGF16

THUD & BLUNDER

THE NOT-SO-HEROIC KNIGHT

Written by
BLAKE HOENA

Illustrated by
POL CUNYAT

STONE ARCH BOOKS
a capstone imprint

Thud is the daughter of the town's blacksmith. She's skilled with a hammer, whether she's pounding out dings in Blunder's armor or thumping a monster. Thud is equal parts brains and brawn!

THE TOWER & FOREST

What **Blunder** lacks in size and smarts, he makes up for in foolishness. He fearlessly charges into danger, whether it's real or not. He wields his mighty broad sword and never backs down from a monster.

CHAPTER 1

A RUMP AND A HUM

The year was Twelvity-Five A.D. Thud and Blunder were at home on a sunny Sunday in Village Town.

When the pair of nine-year-old knights weren't adventuring, they were preparing for adventure. Thud hammered out dents in their armor.

CLANG!

      CLANG!

            CLANG!

Blunder helped by not getting in the way. But that task turned out to be difficult for him.

"You missed one," Blunder said, pointing to the tiniest of dings in a piece of his armor.

Thud grumbled, "I don't know why —"

CLANG!

"— you can't fix —"

CLANG!

"— your own armor!"

CLANG!

A moment later, a **CLIP! CLAP! CLOP!** was heard off in the distance. Blunder jumped up from his seat. He tilted his head and listened.

Thud hammered again. Once more, her clangs were followed by **CLIP! CLAP! CLOP!** Blunder feared it was a monster.

"Quit hammering so loud," Blunder warned. "There's an Echo."

"An Echo?" Thud asked.

"Oh, no, did you hear it?" Blunder shouted.

His eyes darted about as he looked for danger.

Thud looked too. But she didn't see any. Not even a tiny danger.

"Hear what?" Thud asked.

"The Echo," Blunder said.

"The Echo?" Thud asked.

"There it is again!" Blunder shouted.

Blunder drew his sword and got into
his fighting stance. He sort of looked
like a chicken hopping around on one
foot and waving a sword over his head.

"It found us!" Blunder shouted.

"What's found us?" Thud asked, scratching her head with her hammer.

"The Ech—"

A **CLIP! CLAP! CLOP!** interrupted Blunder. The sound came from just down the road. And whoever (or whatever) made the noise was **CLIP-CLAP-CLOPPING** their way toward the nine-year-old knights.

Thud and Blunder ran outside. They watched as a rider approached.

"Could it be a knight?" Blunder asked, squinting.

"I can't tell," Thud said. She had to squint too.

The shine of the person's armor was blinding. They couldn't clearly see who (or what) was riding their way. They just heard a **CLIP! CLAP! CLOP!** getting closer and closer.

The rider stopped in front of them with a **"WHOA!"** Then they heard the screeching of hooves.

SCRREEEEEECH!

"Good day, young sire. Good day, milady," the rider greeted Thud and Blunder.

"He talks funny, like a knight," Thud whispered to Blunder.

"We're knights," Blunder said, "and we don't talk like that."

"But we're nine," Thud added. "Wait until we're old like him. We'll talk funny like that too."

Thud and Blunder cupped their
hands over their eyes and squinted up
at the knight in shining armor.

"Hey," Thud said.

"Yo!" Blunder said.

In gleaming grace, the knight pointed
to where Thud had leaned her hammer
against an anvil.

"I heard the sound of yonder hammering, and —" the knight began.

"Wait. What does *yonder* mean?" Blunder interrupted.

"It's a fancy way of saying 'over there'," Thud whispered into his ear.

The knight continued, "— and I find myself in need of your assistance on my quest."

Thud and Blunder's eyes lit up at the word *quest*. That meant adventure!

"We can help," Thud said.

"We just need a get a few things," Blunder added.

The pair quickly ran back to the house. Thud grabbed her shield and hammer. Blunder started pulling on his armor.

"No, no, you misunderstood," the knight said as he got off his steed. He leaned toward the pair and whispered, "I wasn't asking you to join me. It's just that I . . . um . . . had a bit of trouble with my armor. See!"

For them to truly see, the knight spun around and stuck out his rump.

"My culet has been dented," the knight explained.

Blunder leaned into Thud. "What's a culet?" he asked.

"His buttocks armor," Thud said.

The backside of the knight's armor rounded inward, not outward. It forced him to walk somewhat like a penguin.

"I can't be waddling around court like this," the knight said. And to show them what he meant, he waddled around in front of them. "So I am in need of your aid."

Thud agreed to help, and the knight removed the dented piece of armor.

"How did this happen?" Thud asked. She hoped to hear a tale of danger and heroic deeds.

"Were you kicked by a gigantic giant?" Blunder asked.

"Or attacked by some gobbling goblins?" Thud asked.

The knight shook his head as he handed the piece of armor to Thud.

"No, no," he whispered. "It's because of my trusty steed."

For the first time, Thud and Blunder got a good look at what the knight was riding. It was not a horse, but a camel — the one-humped kind.

CHAPTER 2

A POINTLESS STEED

Thud went to work with her hammer.

CLANG!

> **CLANG!**

>> **CLANG!**

Blunder helped by pointing out the dings she missed.

Thud grumbled, "I don't — **CLANG!** — need any of — **CLANG!** — your help!"

CLANG!

The knight stood by and watched.

Once finished, Thud handed the culet back to the knight.

The knight put it on and then mounted his camel. He sat atop its

hump for a brief second. But slowly
he began to tip one way. Then he tilted
another. And finally — **THUMP!** He
slid off and landed on the ground.

The knight stood and looked from
the camel's hump to the new dent on
his rump.

"Maybe," the knight said. "My steed needs to be more trusty and less tipsy."

"You could borrow ours," Blunder said.

"But only if you take us with you," Thud added.

The knight looked at the two nine-year-olds. He scrunched up his face as he thought and thunk a bit.

"You could be my squires," he finally said.

"What do squires do?" Thud asked.

"They are knights in training," the knight said. "So you will carry my things and tell me how heroic I am. Oh, and you will lay down your lives for me in the dangerest of dangers. So I can get away."

"Is that what squires really do?" Blunder asked Thud.

She shrugged her shoulders. The tasks didn't bother her — or Blunder, for that matter. Both of them wanted to go adventuring more than anything.

"So where is this steed you speak of?" the knight asked.

"Eliot!" Thud shouted.

Soon, they heard **CLIPPITY! CLAPPITY! CLOPPITY!** approaching. Eliot pranced into view.

"Is that your horse?" the knight asked.

Eliot reared up on his hind legs. **"NEIGH!"** he neighed.

"Well, whose horse is it?" the knight asked.

"He didn't neigh about not being ours," Thud said.

"Whatever is he neighing about then?" asked the knight.

"He's neighing about being a horse," Blunder said.

The knight looked at his two new squires and scratched his head.

"Then what is he, if not a horse?" the knight asked.

"A unicorn, of course," Thud stated.

"But he's pointless," the knight pointed out.

Suddenly, Eliot spun around to face the knight. He pawed at the ground with his hooves and flared his nostrils. The knight gulped.

"Just because he's hornless does not mean he's pointless. You'd better take that back," Blunder warned. "Or you might have more than dented buttocks when Eliot is through with you."

"I think he meant a dented culet," Thud said. "Not to sound impolite."

The knight bowed to the unicorn. "Eliot, you are the noblest of steeds. You are not pointless, even though you have no horn."

Eliot snorted and then tossed his mane back gloriously.

"I guess you're forgiven," Blunder said. "So now let's get on this quest."

"First, let me finish packing!" Thud said. She was stuffing some things into her pack.

"What more do you need than your hammer and shield?" Blunder asked.

Thud held up a big squeeze bottle of yellow mustard. "Condiments!"

"Condiments?" the knight asked.

"Oh no, it's back!" Blunder shouted as he drew his sword.

"What's back?" the knight asked.

"The Echo!" Blunder shouted.

"The Echo?" the knight asked, drawing his sword, too.

"The Echo," Thud sighed.

As the knight and Blunder posed heroically with their swords, Thud kept packing.

She stuffed bottles of ketchup and mustard into her pack. Quest food was always a little disgusting. You simply ate whatever you could find, like grubs and pinecones. So condiments were a must.

"We're ready!" Thud shouted a moment later.

Not seeing an Echo, Blunder and the knight sheathed their swords.

Then the knight mounted Eliot. He had never ridden a hornless unicorn before. It took several tries in which he was thrown off, kicked off, or simply fell off before he managed to stay on.

When he was finally ready, Thud and Blunder cupped their hands over their eyes and squinted up at the knight in shining armor.

"Can you make your armor less shiny?" Blunder asked. "I can't stand to look at you anymore."

"And every evil creature in the realm will see you coming," Thud added.

"I know, spectacular, is it not?" the knight said proudly. "But I can turn down the shine for stealthiness."

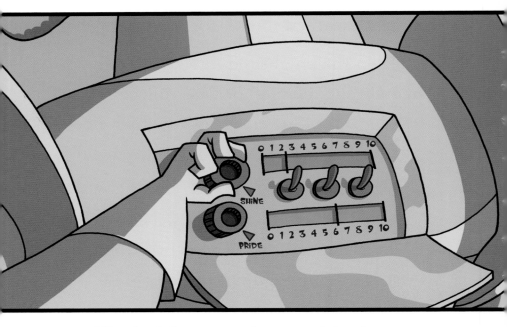

The knight opened a panel in the armor plating on his chest. There were buttons of all sorts. He turned one knob, labeled **SHINE**, down from 8 to 2. His armor went from shining to a dull glow.

"Better?"

CHAPTER 3

QUESTWARD HO!

The knight rode Eliot out of Village Town. Thud and Blunder followed on foot. They carried all of the knight's gear, from extra lances to foot powder.

"Where are we off to?" Blunder groaned under the weight.

The knight held his head high as he proudly stated, "I am on a quest for fame."

Thud and Blunder gave each other a questioning look.

"Aren't quests about battling fearsome beasts?" Thud asked.

"Fame is just the boring part that comes after the monsters are defeated," Blunder added.

"Hmmm, I never thought of it that way," the knight said, placing a hand on his chin. "So how to get fame?"

Thud and Blunder thought about the dangers in the realm.

"We could go to Mount Mountain. A fire-breathing dragon lives up there," Thud suggested.

The knight shook his head. "No. I'm allergic to fire. It gives me blisters."

"What about Castle Kidnapt?" Blunder asked. "A princess is held captive by an crabby ogre."

Again, the knight shook his head. "No, no. I can't have an ogre denting my armor. I won't look good at court when I show off my fame."

Eliot snorted and whinnied.

"Oh yeah, what about The Tower of Evil in the Forest?" Thud suggested.

"The Evil wizard, with a capital *E*, lives there," Blunder added.

"No, no, and NO!" said the knight. "Wizards are such a bore. They are always spelling things."

Blunder drew his sword and waved it about. He pretended to battle an imaginary monster. "But defeating evil is the funnest part of adventuring," Blunder said.

"I'm hoping to skip the dangerous stuff," the knight admitted. "I want to get straight to the fame part."

Thud and Blunder weren't sure of the knight's plan. Going on this quest didn't sound as heroic as they had hoped.

"But if you don't do heroic deeds," Thud said, "you won't get invited to meet the king. And you won't get to go to a ball, where you can brag of your heroic deeds."

"Don't you have to dance at balls?" Blunder asked.

The knight leaped off of Eliot with surprising grace. Then on his tippiest toe, which was the big toe on his right foot, he spun around several times.

"I am a master dancer," said the knight. He leaped and skipped about. "I have the heart of a ballerina and wish to go to balls. Truthfully, I'm only questing so that I get invited to one. But first, I need fame."

"Then what should we do for a quest?" Thud asked.

"I have an idea," the knight said.

He stopped mid-pirouette and pointed into the distance. There was an area ahead where the forest simply withered away. It was a desert wasteland surrounded by towering mountains.

"The Sand Witch's lair?" Thud asked.

"Yes," the knight said. "I hear she's just an old hag. I doubt she'll put up much of a fight."

"So we aren't seeking fame in battle?" Thud asked, disappointed.

The knight shook his head.

"Then what type of fame are we after?" Blunder asked.

"Wealth will be our key to fame," the knight said. "I have heard there are untold treasures in the Sand Witch's lair."

The knight smiled proudly. He thought it was a brilliant idea. That is, until Thud asked, "What about the monsters guarding the entrance to her lair?"

The knight gulped. "Nobody said anything about monsters. They just talked about the Sand Witch's treasures."

"For starters, there are strangling spiky vines," Thud said.

"Then there are the gobs of gooey goo," Blunder added.

The knight thought about what the pair was telling him.

"This is why a knight has squires," he boldly said. "You'll take care of the non-important monsters. You know, the ones I'm too heroic to battle, like spiky vines and gooey goo."

As he said that, they reached the Sand Witch's lair. The entrance was a locked grate in the ground, surrounded by scraggly vines.

As they walked up to the entrance, the vines around them began to twist and quiver and snarl.

"What is that?" the knight gulped as a vine crept toward Eliot's hoof.

Blunder drew his sword. He quickly sliced up the vine.

"That is a spiky vine," Thud said.

"Well, I will sit atop my steed as you take care of them," the knight said.

At least that's what he said. What happened was Eliot reared up on his hind legs. The knight slid from his saddle and landed on the ground with a thump!

Eliot pranced safely away as the vines attacked.

TWANG! Thud blocked a vine with her shield. Then she smashed it with her hammer. **THUMP!** The flattened vine slowly slithered away.

SLICE! SLICE! Blunder swung his sword. He cut several vines to pieces.

"Help!" the knight cried.

Vines had wrapped themselves
around his legs and arms. He was being
pulled in four different directions.

"I will bash open the gate," Thud said, lifting up her hammer.

"I will cut the knight free," Blunder said, raising his sword above his head.

BANG!

SLICE!

CLANG!

HACK!

The grate leading to the Sand Witch's lair was busted open. The knight had been cut free. But the three of them were still surround by spiky vines.

So they all leaped through the grate and landed with a **THUD**.

"Now, what about those gobs of gooey goo?" the knight asked.

CHAPTER 4

KETCHUP AND MUSTARD

"I can't see a thing," Blunder grumbled.

"Turn up the shine on your armor," Thud told the knight.

The knight opened the panel on his chest and turned the knob to 5. That gave them enough shine to see. Not that they wanted to see what was around them.

Gobs of gooey goo hung from the ceiling. Mounds of quivering goo rose up from the floor and slowly oozed toward them. Goo seeped from the tunnel walls.

"EW!" the knight shrieked.

A drop of goo dripped on his armor. The spot where it landed began to sizzle and hiss.

"The goo is like acid," Thud shouted.

The three of them huddled close as the goo oozed around them.

"Maybe we can climb out," the knight said, looking up.

SLAM! A spiky vine slammed the grate closed above them.

"Or not," Blunder said.

"That leaves only one option," the knight said.

"And what's that?" Thud asked.

In answer to her question, the knight raised his hands above his head. He began to shriek as loudly as he could. Then he ran down the tunnel. He burst right through the gooey goo.

Thud and Blunder quickly followed. The not-so-heroic knight had cleared a path for them.

Goo sizzled and hissed as it clung to the knight. But his armor did the trick. It protected the knight.

But by time they were past the goo, there wasn't much left of the knight's armor — just a few straps and bolts and a couple thin strips of metal.

It all clattered to the ground once the knight stopped running. All that remained was his helmet. He was left standing in his pink prancing pony underpants.

Thud and Blunder looked in amazement — not at the knight's pink prancing pony underpants — but at what they saw in front of them. They were now in a large room. Treasure chests were stacked up against one wall.

The knight walked over to the chests. As he reached to open one of them, a hand made of sand rose up from the sandy floor. It slapped the knight's hand away.

"Don't touch my treasure," a voice wheezed behind them.

They all turned to see an old woman covered in rags. She had a large nose with a hairy mole that looked somewhat like a hungry spider. When she spoke, she coughed out sand.

"It's the Sand Witch!" Thud and Blunder shouted at the same time.

Thud hefted her hammer. Blunder drew his sword. They charged as the knight tiptoed away in the opposite direction.

Sand hands darted out from the walls and ceiling. One snatched Thud's hammer. Another knocked her shield away. A sand hand wrestled Blunder's sword out of his grasp. Two more sand hands grabbed the knight's feet and tripped him.

"Now that you have found my lair, I can't let you leave," the Sand Witch wheezed and coughed.

Sand hands surrounded them. They stuck out from the floor, walls, and ceiling.

"Now what?" Blunder asked.

"We need a distraction!" Thud shouted.

Just then, the knight gracefully leaped away from the sand hands that

47

reached for him. He spun and twirled and started to nae nae.

Sand hands reached from the ceiling, darted up from the floor, and shot out from the walls. But the knight's dance moves were too graceful. He kept getting away from their grasp.

With the Sand Witch distracted, Thud reached into her sack and pulled out the squeeze bottles of condiments. She handed one to Blunder.

"What do you want me to do with this?" he asked.

"Nothing ruins a Sand Witch like too many condiments!" Thud shouted.

Then she squeezed her bottle. Mustard sprayed all over the room and the Sand Witch.

"EEK!" she shrieked.

Blunder squeezed his bottle of ketchup.

"EW!" the Sand Witch screamed.

Soon everything was covered and dripping in mustard and ketchup. The sand hands stopped attacking. They were too busy trying to shake off the gunk that covered them.

Thud walked over and picked her hammer off the ground. Blunder grabbed his sword.

"Now what?" the knight asked.

"To victory!" Blunder cried.

"And battle!" Thud added.

The Sand Witch turned and ran.

Thud and Blunder charged after her. The knight leaped after them.

"And fame," he shouted. "Don't forget the fame!"

Talk about the Tale!

1. A pun is a joke about the different meanings for a word or phrase. An example is the Sand Witch, who Thud and Blunder cover with condiments, just like you would a sandwich. What other puns can you find in this story?

2. Thud and Blunder disagree with the knight on how to get fame. How do Thud and Blunder think you achieve fame? The Knight? Who do you agree with?

3. The knight loves to dance. Why do you think he is going on quests like a knight instead dancing at balls like a dancer?

Write about the Adventure!

1. This story is about a not-so-heroic knight. Imagine that he met a not-so-fearsome beast. First, describe the beast. Then write a story about what happens.

2. At different parts in the story, Blunder hears an echo and thinks it is a monster. If an echo really was a monster, what would it look like? What abilities would it have? Write a story about Thud and Blunder facing the Echo.

3. At the end of the story, Thud and Blunder chase after the Sand Witch. But what happens next? Write a new ending for the story, telling what happens to the Sand Witch.

GLOSSARY

court—the place where kings, queens, and noble people meet to listen to knights brag about their heroic deeds

culet—piece of armor covering a knight's buttocks

hag—a witch, often an old-looking one with a big hairy mole on her nose

lair—a special place where someone hides

milady—an old-fashioned and polite way of greeting a woman (or a girl)

quest—just like an adventure, though with the purpose of seeking fame and glory

realm—kingdom

sire—an old-fashioned, respectful way of greeting a man (or a boy)

squire—a knight in training; basically someone who takes care of knights' needs, like carrying all of their stuff and telling them that they are really brave

steed—an animal that someone rides, most often a horse or camel, but possibly a hornless unicorn in you are an adventurer

ABOUT THE CREATORS

ABOUT the AUTHOR

Author Blake Hoena grew up in central Wisconsin, where he wrote stories about robots conquering the moon and trolls lumbering around the woods behind his parents' house. He now lives in St. Paul, Minnesota, with his wife, two kids, two dogs, and a cat. Blake continues to make up stories about things like space aliens, superheroes, and monsters.

ABOUT the ILLUSTRATOR

Illustrator Pol Cunyat was born in 1979 in Sant Celoni, a small village near Barcelona, Spain. As a child, Pol always dreamed of being an illustrator. So he went to study illustration in Escola De Còmic Joso de Barcelona and Escola D'Art, Serra i Abella de L'Hospitalet. Now, Pol makes a living doing illustration work for various publishers and studios. Pol's dream has come true, but he will never stop dreaming.

Check out more
THUD & BLUNDER
Adventures!

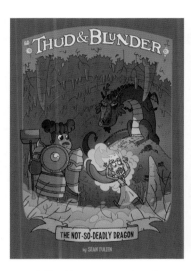

THE NOT-SO-DEADLY DRAGON

by SEAN TULIEN

THE NOT-SO-HEROIC KNIGHT

by BLAKE HOENA

THE NOT-SO-HELPLESS PRINCESS

by BLAKE HOENA

THE NOT-SO-EVIL WIZARD

by SEAN TULIEN

For MORE GREAT BOOKS go to
WWW.MYCAPSTONE.COM